A Kooties Club MYSTERY

Membership Card

Name

Nickname

School

Age

Permission is granted by the publisher to reproduce the Kooties Club Membership Card

The Mystery of the Thief That Nobody Noticed

by M. J. Cosson

Perfection Learning®

Cover and Inside Illustrations: Michael A. Aspengren

For information, contact
Perfection Learning® Corporation,
1000 North Second Avenue, P.O. Box 500,
Logan, Iowa 51546-0500.
Tel: 1-800-831-4190
Fax: 1-712-644-2392

1 2 3 4 5 6 PP 09 08 07 06 05 04

Paperback ISBN 0-7891-6436-1
Cover Craft® ISBN 0-7569-3492-3

Table of Contents

Introduction

Abe, Ben, Gabe, Toby, and Ty live
in a large city. There isn't much for
kids to do. There isn't even a park
close by.

Their neighborhood is made up of apartment houses and trailer parks. Gas stations and small shops stand where the parks and grass used to be. And there aren't many houses with big yards.

Ty and Abe live in an apartment complex. Next door is a large vacant lot. It is full of brush, weeds, and trash. A path runs across the lot. On the other side is a trailer park. Ben and Toby live there.

Across the street from the trailer park is a big gray house. Gabe lives in the top apartment of the house.

The five boys have known one another since they started school. But they haven't always been friends.

The other kids say the boys have cooties. And the other kids won't touch them with a ten-foot pole. So Abe, Ben, Gabe, Toby, and Ty have formed their own club. They call it the Kooties Club.

Here's how to join. If no one else will have anything to do with you, you're in.

The boys call themselves the Koots for short. Ben's grandma calls his grandpa an *old coot.* And Ben thinks his grandpa is pretty cool. So if he's an old coot, Ben and his friends must be young koots.

The Koots play ball and hang out with one another. But most of all, they look for mysteries to solve.

Chapter 1

Pay Attention, Gabe!

"Gabe! Gabe, please keep your pencil quiet," Ms. Morris said.

Gabe looked up. He was playing a song in his head and tapping his pencil on his desk. He had no idea what was going on in class.

Ms. Morris gave Gabe the look. The look told Gabe that he would probably miss recess again.

"Who can show us how to find the answer for 42 minus 27?" Ms. Morris asked. "Good, Tara, come up and show us on the board."

Gabe's mind went back to the song. He had heard it on the radio that morning. He was trying to remember the words. He started tapping his pencil again.

A hand stopped his pencil from tapping. Gabe looked up. Ms. Morris was bending over him. Gabe couldn't understand what she was saying. It wasn't making sense. Gabe tried to concentrate.

"Gabe, please pay attention. This is mathematics, not music," Ms. Morris said.

"I'm trying," Gabe said. "But I have this song in my head."

"Get rid of the song, Gabe," Ms. Morris said. "Put math in your head."

Gabe tried to think of math. The song kept coming back, though.

Gabe stayed in from recess to work on his math. He never finished it in class. It wasn't just math either. He was behind in every subject. Gabe hardly ever went to recess anymore.

After school, the Koots walked home.

"This morning my mom was talking to our neighbor, Mrs. Gomez," Ben said.

"So? My mom talks to our neighbors all the time," Ty said.

"I wasn't done," Ben said. "Mrs. Gomez had something stolen from her house."

"Hey, my neighbor Mrs. Wu told my mom that she was missing something too. A picture from a wall in her living room is gone," Abe said. "My mom thought it was strange that someone would take a picture."

"What was the picture of?" Toby asked.

13

"Flowers. I think somebody painted it. I've seen it. It's not very big," Abe said.

"What did Mrs. Gomez lose?" Ty asked.

"I don't know," Ben said. "I'll have to find out."

"Maybe we have a thief in the neighborhood," Toby said.

"Yeah, maybe we have a mystery," Ben said.

Now that school was out, Gabe was thinking about math. He was doing math problems in his head. But when Gabe heard the word "mystery," he forgot about math.

"Mystery?" Gabe said. "We have a mystery?"

"Pay attention, Gabe," Toby said. "We may have a mystery to solve."

14

Chapter 2

Three Thefts

After dinner, the Koots met on Gabe's front porch.

"I found out from my mom that Mrs. Gomez lost a very old vase. She kept it on her coffee table. It had belonged to her mother. It was very important to her. She saw that it was missing last night," Ben said.

"Mrs. Wu's picture has been missing for at least two days," Abe said.

"I heard about something else that's missing," Toby said. "Mrs. Purdy is missing an old doll. It sat on a chair in her living room. She says it is worth a lot of money. She is very upset. It's been gone for three days."

"Wow, three things missing. I think we have a case," Ty said.

"What should we do to solve this mystery?" Gabe asked.

Ben thought a minute. "What do these missing things have in common?"

"They're all old," Toby said.

"They were in people's houses," Abe said.

16

"They are worth something. Maybe not a lot of money. But a bunch of things worth a little money adds up to a lot of money," Gabe said.

"There's a pattern!" Ben yelled. Everyone looked at him. "One a day. The doll went missing three days ago. The picture was taken two days ago. The vase was stolen last night."

"What will happen tonight?" Abe asked.

"We need a plan," Ben said.

"We need to keep our eyes and ears open," Ty said.

"I always keep my eyes open when I'm awake. And my ears can't close," Abe said.

"It's a saying, Abe," the Koots said together.

17

"It means we need to be on the lookout," Ty said.

"Let's walk around. We'll see what we can see," Toby said.

The Koots walked around the neighborhood for two hours. Most people were in their houses. A few people sat outside. A jogger in blue shorts ran by. Some kids played tag.

One guy was sticking fliers in people's doors.

"Maybe he tests the doors to see if they're locked. If they're not, he walks in and takes something," Toby said.

The Koots followed the guy with the fliers. After a couple of blocks, he turned around. He looked at the Koots.

"Are you following me?" he asked.

18

"No," the Koots all said together. Except Abe.

"Yes," Abe said.

"Why?" asked the guy. "I'm just doing my job."

"What's your job?" Toby asked.

The guy walked back toward the Koots. "I'm paid by Tony's Pizza to put these fliers in people's doors and on cars. See, it says that if you buy one pizza, you get the second one free. Here, take one."

"We don't have money to buy a pizza," Gabe said.

"Well, give it to your parents," the guy said. "I won't be paid until I get rid of all of these." He handed out fliers and walked away.

"Do you think it's him?" asked Abe.

"Maybe," Ty said. "I think we should watch him."

"It can't be him," Gabe said. "This has happened for at least three nights. That guy can't spend every night in this neighborhood. He has to keep moving to new places."

"True," Ben said. "But maybe things are missing all over town. We only know about this neighborhood."

20

"If we see him tomorrow night, we should tell someone," Toby said.

It was almost 8 o'clock. Time to go inside. Tomorrow was a school day. The Koots walked down the street toward home. Cars and trucks went by on the busy street.

"Who could it be?" Ben asked.

"It could be a lot of different people," Ty said.

"I don't think so," Gabe said. "There's something fishy about all the thefts. They are too much alike. I think it's the same person."

The Koots split up to go to their own homes. They'd have to wait until tomorrow to keep working on the mystery.

21

Chapter 3

Gabe's Problem

"There's been another theft," Toby told the Koots on the way to school. "My brother's friend Sam lost his CD player."

"Where did he lose it?" Ben asked.

"I don't know," Toby said. "He called my brother Todd to see if he had it. But Todd didn't have it. So I think it's been stolen."

"It doesn't fit in with the other things," Gabe said. "It isn't old. And it isn't something people would like to look at."

"You mean like the vase or the painting or the doll," Abe said.

"Exactly," Ben said.

"Hmm," said Ty. "Maybe our thief just grabs whatever he can get his hands on."

The Koots were still wondering about the thief when the school bell rang.

And Gabe was still wondering about the thief during history. He was thinking about the guy who was sticking fliers in people's doors. Would the Koots see him again tonight? If so, what would they do? Follow him?

23

"Gabe!"

Gabe looked up. Ms. Morris had that look on her face.

"Can you tell me the answer, Gabe?" Ms. Morris asked.

"George Washington?"

"We're not talking about George Washington, Gabe," Ms. Morris said. "I'll see you at recess."

At recess, Gabe tried to work on his history worksheet. But he kept thinking of the thief. Ms. Morris sat down in the chair next to his desk.

"Gabe, I've asked your mom to take you to the doctor. You have an appointment after school today."

"Why?" asked Gabe. "I feel fine."

"I've noticed that you've had trouble paying attention for a while now," said Ms. Morris. "And I think a

24

doctor might be able to help you. The doctor will ask you questions about school. You should answer her as best you can."

"Will the questions be hard?" Gabe asked. He had a lot of trouble with hard questions. His mind wandered when he tried to think of the answers.

"The questions won't be hard. They will be about you and the way you learn. You'll do just fine."

25

Gabe thought about the Koots and the mystery. He wouldn't be able to help tonight. He hoped they didn't catch the thief while he was at the doctor's office.

"Do I have a choice?" Gabe asked.

"Your mother already changed her work schedule so she could take you. It's the right thing to do."

"Rats!" Gabe said to himself.

Chapter 4

The Shiny Green Ball

After school, four Koots went home to find out about the missing CD player. Gabe waited for his mom to pick him up.

The doctor seemed nice. Gabe didn't mind talking to her. He did his best to answer her questions. She said she could help Gabe pay attention in school.

Gabe didn't think about the doctor as his mom drove home. Gabe was thinking about the thief. They passed a woman walking her dog and some kids on skateboards.

As they drove by Mrs. Ogden's house, Gabe's spied a shiny green ball in her garden. He knew what he had to do.

Gabe's mom pulled up to their house and parked the car. Gabe jumped out. "I'll be back in a minute," he called.

Gabe had seen a movie where a lady looked into a ball. She was able to tell people what would happen next. Gabe decided he would ask a question of Mrs. Ogden's green ball. He walked into her yard and put a

28

hand on each side of the ball. He put his
face close to it.

"Who is the thief?" Gabe asked.

29

"Thief!" Mrs. Ogden yelled. She ran down her steps. She waved a broom over her head. She was running straight toward Gabe. Gabe looked up. Mrs. Ogden was getting close.

"Thief!" she yelled. She waved the broom. "Get away from my ball! Get out of my yard!"

Gabe backed away. He began to run. "I wasn't going to take it!" he yelled over his shoulder. He kept running all the way home.

• • • • • • • • • • • • • • • • •

"I wasn't going to take the ball," Gabe told the Koots later. "I was just asking it a question. Remember that movie we saw? The lady who found out things from the ball?"

30

"It's not that kind of ball," Toby said. "It's for a garden."

"I know," Gabe said. "But I guess I thought it wouldn't hurt. I've been in Mrs. Ogden's yard before. I've asked that ball questions before.
Mrs. Ogden never used to run after me with a broom."

"My mom says people are scared that they'll have something taken," Ben said. "I guess Mrs. Ogden was afraid you'd take the ball."

"Did the ball ever answer your questions?" Ty asked.

"No," Gabe said.

"Well, then, quit asking it questions," Ben said. "You know balls can't talk."

Gabe felt silly. He wished he hadn't told the Koots about the ball.

The Koots walked around the neighborhood. Again, they didn't see any thieves. They didn't even see the guy with the fliers. They saw a mom pushing a baby stroller. And a man was sitting on a bench feeding some birds.

The next morning Gabe walked to the corner to meet the other Koots. As he passed Mrs. Ogden's house, he stopped. The shiny green ball was gone.

Chapter 5

More Missing!

All day Gabe had trouble paying attention. He worried that the police would come to school. They'd put him in jail for taking Mrs. Ogden's shiny garden ball. But he hadn't taken it. Who had?

Four of the Koots walked past Mrs. Ogden's house on the way home from school. Not Gabe. He took the long way home. He didn't want Mrs. Ogden to yell at him again. He didn't have her green garden ball.

The Koots met Gabe at his front steps.

"Anybody know of any more thefts?" Toby asked.

"Just the ball," Gabe said.

"Did you take it?" Ty asked.

"NO!" Gabe said. He folded his arms and looked mad.

"Well, I don't know of any other thefts," said Ben. "I think we should check the whole neighborhood. We'll ask people what's missing. If something is gone, we'll ask them when it happened."

"And where they last saw it," Abe said.

"And who they think did it," Ty said.

"Good idea," Toby said. "Should we stay together or split up?"

"We'll never get through the neighborhood if we stay together," Ty said. "Abe and I will go to the apartments. Toby, you and Ben check the trailer court. Gabe, you check the houses on this block."

"I'm not checking Mrs. Ogden's. She'll run after me with a broom again. And why am I the only one who has to be by myself?" Gabe asked.

"Okay, I'll ask Mrs. Ogden," Toby said.

35

Ben said, "I'll check the houses across the street. Gabe, you go that way. Then all three of us will check the trailer court. We'll all meet at my trailer in an hour. Okay?"

Everybody gave the Kootie handshake. Then the Koots went off to ask neighbors if they'd been robbed.

At 5:30, the Koots met at Ben's trailer.

"Does anybody have anything new?" Gabe asked.

"Sam found his CD player under his bed," Toby said. "So it's not part of the mystery."

"The Cooks lost a clock," Ben said. "It's been gone about a week."

36

"Mr. Hoang is missing a small chess set. It was on his coffee table," Toby said.

"The Ruiz family lost a glass candy dish. It was full of candy too," Abe said. "They noticed that it was gone just this morning."

"Anything else?" Gabe asked.

Toby cleared his throat. "Mrs. Ogden's ball," he said.

Gabe's shoulders got stiff. "What about it?" he asked.

"Well, it's not in the garden," Toby said. "So I asked Mrs. Ogden." He was taking his time. "She said she was afraid it would be stolen." He cleared his throat. "So she took it inside."

Toby smiled.

Gabe sighed. At least that was one thing he wouldn't be in trouble for.

Chapter 6

A Clue

The Koots spent the rest of the
evening putting their notes together.

"I don't see any pattern," Ben said.

"None of the things are even
alike," Toby said.

"Well, one thing is the same.
Nobody thinks that anyone broke in,"
Abe said.

"Maybe nobody stole anything. Maybe all these things are just lost. You know, like Sam's CD player," Ty said.

"No," said Gabe. "There are too many. And you don't lose a picture that's hanging on a wall. Or a candy dish full of candy."

The Koots went to bed that night wondering what happened to the picture, the vase, the doll, the clock, the chess set, and the candy dish. How were they alike?

Just as he was about to fall asleep, Abe sat up in bed. He had a clue! He couldn't wait until morning to tell the rest of the Koots.

"There's a pattern," Abe said on the way to school. "Where did all the thefts take place? Every theft was either in the apartments or the trailer court. Nothing is missing from the houses."

"Hmmm," Ty said. "You're right! We thought the ball was missing. But now we know it's safe. That was the only thing missing from a house."

"What's different about the houses?" Ben asked.

"They're big," Abe said.

"They're older than the apartments or the trailers," Ty said.

"Mostly old people live in them," Abe said.

"What do you think, Gabe? What's different?" Ben asked.

"What?" Gabe asked. He had been thinking about his doctor's appointment. He was thinking about what he had learned about himself. He couldn't think about the thefts too.

41

Chapter 7

Ask Mr. Dodge

It was Friday. That meant the Koots could stay up late. They planned what they would do as they walked home from school.

"Let's get a big piece of paper and draw all the places on it. You know, the ones that have lost something," Ben said.

42

"I think we should talk more to the people who have been robbed," Toby said.

"I like Ben's idea," Ty said.

"What do you think, Gabe?" Ben asked.

"What?" Gabe asked. "Oh, I think that's a good idea."

"Which one?" Ty asked.

"The first one," Gabe said.

Ben and Ty looked at each other.

"What's wrong, Gabe?" Ty asked.

"Nothing," Gabe said.

Nobody said anything for a while.

"How about pizza?" Abe said. "I gave my dad that flier. I think I can get him to order a pizza. And we'll get one free. There will be plenty for everyone."

43

"Sounds good!" everybody said.

Two hours later, the Koots were watching TV at Abe's apartment. They were full of pizza. Now Abe's mom was making popcorn.

"Maybe we should ask Mr. Dodge about the thefts," Ben said.

"Sure, he can probably guess who did it. We should have thought of that before," Ty said.

44

"Let's go see him tomorrow morning," Gabe said. "I'll come over about 9."

"Me too," said Ben.

"Me too," said Ty.

"Me too," said Toby.

"See you guys then," Abe said. He was just finishing the popcorn.

Chapter 8

We've Been Robbed!

The next morning when the Koots got to Abe's house, they had a surprise.

"We've been robbed!" Abe said.

"What's missing?" Ty asked. He looked around the room.

"My mom had a key holder on the wall by the kitchen. It isn't worth

enough to bother the police. But it came from India. Mom feels pretty bad that it's gone."

"What does it look like?" Toby asked.

"It's gold, but not real gold. It has hooks on it. It is very fancy," Abe said.

"Oh, I've seen it," Ty said. The Koots had all seen the key holder.

"Were any keys on it?" Ben asked.

Abe shook his head. "No keys," he said.

"That's good," Ben said. "At least the thief can't take your car or come in here when you're gone."

"When did you last see it?" Gabe asked.

"It's one of those things you get used to," Abe said. "It might have been gone for many days. Mom just noticed when she went to put her keys on it this morning. They had been in her purse."

"Let's go see Mr. Dodge," Ty said. "Maybe he'll know what to do."

Mr. Dodge had some advice.

"Look for patterns," he said.

"We have," said the Koots.

"Draw it out on paper," he said.

"We have," said the Koots.

"Keep thinking about it. Keeping asking people for clues," he said.

"We are," said the Koots.

"Sometimes it's somebody you know," Mr. Dodge said. "Don't rule out neighbors. It could be someone who lives right here."

Ben nodded. "That's a good idea. We need to watch the neighbors too."

Mr. Dodge said. "I have a new mystery on tape. Do you want to listen to it?"

So the Koots listened to Mr. Dodge's mystery. It was called "The Case of the Bloody Hand."

Gabe tried to listen. He always tried to listen to Mr. Dodge's mysteries. All the other Koots enjoyed them so much. But it was hard for Gabe to pay attention for such a long time.

Chapter 9

More Questions

Late Saturday afternoon, the Koots talked to the neighbors again. They watched for patterns. They looked around to see if the neighbors had something that didn't belong to them. Like a candy dish or a picture.

The Koots were walking from Mrs. Purdy's trailer to Mrs. Gomez's trailer.

"Mrs. Purdy is sure the doll disappeared a week ago today. She said her son had stopped by for supper," Toby said.

"Maybe her son took the doll," Ty said.

"Why would he do that?" Ben asked.

"I don't know. But we can't rule out anyone," Ty said.

All the Koots were talking, but Gabe was only hearing noise. He walked along and looked around the trailer court. A dog barked, pulling his attention down the street. Something was going on a few trailers down. It was something he saw all the time, but this time he watched closely.

The Koots knocked on Mrs.
Gomez's door. No answer.

Gabe kept watching down the
street.

Finally the door opened. "Hi, boys," Mrs. Gomez said. "Is this about the vase again?"

"Yes," Toby said. "May we ask you a few more questions?"

"Sure. Come on in," Mrs. Gomez said.

"I'll wait out here," Gabe said. He sat down on Mrs. Gomez's steps. He kept looking down the street.

Ten minutes later when the Koots came out, Gabe said, "The mystery is solved."

"What? How?" the Koots all asked.

"Let me just check one thing," Gabe said. He walked down the street. He stopped at Mrs. Purdy's house. He knocked on the door.

Mrs. Purdy opened the door. "Back again!" she said.

53

Gabe said, "I have one more question for you, Mrs. Purdy. What did you give your son for dinner last week?"

"Let me see," Mrs. Purdy said. She put her hand on her cheek. "Oh yes, I ordered that special from Tony's Pizza. Two for one. It came right before my son came over. It was quite good. Why?"

"Did you have the money to pay for the pizza when it got here?" Gabe asked.

"What a funny question. Let me think," Mrs. Purdy said. "No, I had to go find my purse."

"What did the pizza guy look like?" Gabe asked.

"Oh, it was a nice young woman. She wore baggy clothes. They were too big for her. I gave her a nice tip."

Gabe said, "I think she took your doll."

Chapter 10

Gabe Comes Clean

"How did you guess?" Ben asked.

"When you were talking to Mrs. Gomez, I saw a Tony's Pizza car down the street. The driver was a lady in baggy clothes. She was at that trailer." Gabe pointed down the street. "When she came back out, she took something from under her top. She put it in the car."

"Let's go see if anything is missing," Toby said.

The Koots ran down the street. They knocked on the door. It opened.

"Yes?" the man at the door said.

"Excuse me, sir," Ty said. "Did you just have something stolen?"

"What? No, we're eating right now," the man said.

"Yes, we know," Toby said.

"You just had pizza delivered," Gabe said.

"Don't you boys have anything better to do than spy on neighbors?" the man asked. He slammed the door.

The Koots looked at each other. They sat down on the man's front steps and waited.

57

Two minutes later, the door opened.

"My camera is gone. It was sitting on the kitchen table," the man said. "How did you know?"

Gabe told the man what he had seen. Toby told him about the other thefts. Abe told him about ordering pizza last night and losing the key holder.

"It must be that young woman. I'm sure Tony's Pizza doesn't know about this. I think it's time to call the police," the man said. "You boys wait right here."

The Koots sat back down on the steps.

"How did you figure it out?" Ben asked Gabe.

58

"Well," Gabe said. "You know how it's hard for me to pay attention when someone is talking? Sometimes I am paying attention. Just not to what everyone else is paying attention to. When you were talking, I was watching the pizza car."

"How did you know to?" Ben asked.

"I didn't. I just started watching it," Gabe said. "I have something called A-D-D."

"What's that?" Abe asked.

"I don't remember what it stands for. But it makes it hard for me to pay attention. I've been to the doctor. She says she can help me."

"Well, it seems to have helped you solve the mystery, so it's a good thing," Toby said.

"It can be a bad thing too," Gabe said. "But I'm going to learn to live with it." He smiled.

As the police car pulled up, the Koots all gave the Kootie handshake.

Another mystery solved.